School Trip for Superheroes

By **Jenny Moore**

Illustrated by **Daniel Limon**

The children at Swooptown School for Superheroes were super excited about their trip to the museum.

"Quiet now," called Mrs Wonder. "I need to tell you the rules before we leave."

The children groaned.

"No running off in the museum," Mrs Wonder told them. "We need to stay together."

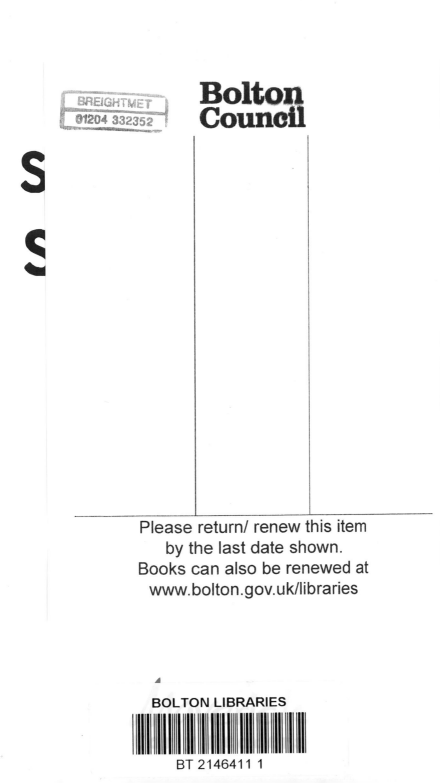

**Bolton
Council**

S

S

Please return/ renew this item
by the last date shown.
Books can also be renewed at
www.bolton.gov.uk/libraries

'School Trip for Superheroes'
An original concept by Jenny Moore
© Jenny Moore

Illustrated by Daniel Limon

Published by MAVERICK ARTS PUBLISHING LTD

Studio 11, City Business Centre, 6 Brighton Road,

Horsham, West Sussex, RH13 5BB

© Maverick Arts Publishing Limited February 2021

+44 (0)1403 256941

A CIP catalogue record for this book is available at the British Library.

ISBN 978-1-84886-766-6

Maverick
publishing

www.maverickbooks.co.uk

Purple

This book is rated as: Purple Band (Guided Reading)

"No running?" said Zoom, looking fed up.

"And no shouting," added Mrs Wonder.

"NO SHOUTING?" yelled Boom Boy, making the classroom walls shake.

Mrs Wonder pretended not to hear.

"And no using your superpowers in public," she finished.

The children groaned even louder.

"I mean it," said Mrs Wonder. "Remember, the Superhero Code says that all powers must be kept secret. I'm sure we can manage without them for one day."

Vanish put up his hand. "I can't control my power," he said. "Sometimes I turn invisible for no reason."

Mrs Wonder smiled. "I know. Just do your best," she told him. "I'm sure it will be fine."

The museum was busy.

"Get down," Mrs Wonder told Flutter, grabbing her jumper. "No flying on the stairs. No flying anywhere."

"Sorry Mrs Wonder, I got excited," Flutter replied. She quickly floated down.

An old man behind them blinked in shock and rubbed his eyes. "I must be seeing things," he said. "Perhaps I need new glasses."

Mrs Wonder looked hot and bothered when they finally reached the Egyptian mummies. "Time for a quick head count," she said. "Four… five… six…" She counted again. But someone was still missing. "Oh no. Has anyone seen Vanish?"

The children shook their heads.

"Vanish?" Mrs Wonder called. "He could be anywhere," she groaned. "We'll have to go back and find him."

"Okay!" said Zoom, rushing off before Mrs Wonder could stop him.

"Yoo-hoo!" called the other children, patting at thin air. "Are you there?"

"COOOOEEEE!" roared Boom Boy as they passed a group of stuffed animals. The tiger trembled. The lion shook.

"Help!" cried an old lady, diving behind an elephant. "It's an earthquake!"

"No superpowers, remember!" hissed Mrs Wonder.

They finally found Vanish fast asleep on

the back seat of the coach.

"Hello, Mrs Wonder," he yawned, turning

visible again. "Are we there yet?"

Mrs Wonder was looking very hot and bothered by the time they got back to the Egyptian mummies. She fanned her face with some worksheets.

"Don't worry. I'll cool you down,"
said Winter, forgetting about the 'no
superpowers' rule.

Zzzzap! Streams of ice-cold air flew out of
the ends of his fingers.

"Woah!" cried Eagle, pointing at the nearest
mummy. "Look at that!"

Winter was so busy looking at the mummies

that he forgot to switch off his cold air.

By the time he noticed, it was too late.

Mrs Wonder was trapped in a big block of ice!

"Oh no," said Winter, turning pale. "I didn't

mean to do that. I'm so sorry, Mrs Wonder."

But Mrs Wonder didn't answer. She couldn't

move her lips. She couldn't move anything.

She was frozen solid!

"What should we do?" asked Winter. "We

can't leave Mrs Wonder like that. It will take

days for her to thaw out."

"How about a short heat blast to melt the ice?" said Flame. "I can do it now, while no one's watching."

"You'll have to hurry," said Eagle, peering through the museum wall. "Another group of children is just coming in."

Flame pointed at the block of ice. The tips of

her fingers began to glow.

Crackle. Little streams of flame reached towards

the ice.

Sizzle! The ice began to melt. It was working!

"Whoa," cried Eagle, pointing to a carved

Viking stone. "Look at that!"

Flame turned to see, shooting a stray

stream of flame at the chair in the corner.

Beep, beep, beep, beep, beep! The fire alarm

went off as the chair caught light.

"Oh no," cried Flame. "We're in big trouble

now!"

"Don't worry," said Winter. "I'll fix this."

He pointed his fingers at the chair.

Whoosh! Huge jets of cold water shot across the room.

"What are you doing?" gasped Mrs Wonder.

All the ice had melted.

"I'm putting out the fire," said Winter.

But there *was* no fire now. Just a deep puddle filling the room. "Oops, sorry," he said, turning off his jets.

Water dripped off the walls and ceiling.

A lady with a pushchair came into the room.

"Oh my goodness," she cried, staring at the
flood. "It must be a burst pipe."

"Look out," called Eagle. "There's a fire engine on its way." She peered through the floor. "And the museum guards look really angry."

Mrs Wonder sighed. "No superpowers, I said. What a mess! It looks like we'll have to break the rules one more time."

She stretched out her fingers towards the clock on the wall and everything stopped.

The clock hands stopped ticking.

The water stopped dripping. The lady with the pushchair stood frozen in time.

"Ah," said Mrs Wonder. "That's better. Now then," she told the children. "Eagle, I need you to look in the cupboards for a mop and bucket. Zoom, you can ferry the buckets of water down to the drain outside. Flutter, I need you to dry off the ceiling."

"WHAT ABOUT ME?" bellowed Boom Boy.

"WHAT SHALL I DO?"

"You can stay nice and quiet with Vanish, Winter and Flame, while I drink my tea," said Mrs Wonder. She sat down on the wet chair and pulled a flask out of her bag. "And once everything is dry and tidy, we'll try again with our school trip. But no superpowers this time!"

Quiz

1. Where did the children go for their school trip?

a) A beach

b) A nature park

c) A museum

2. Where did they find Vanish?

a) The back of the coach

b) In the gift shop

c) In the cafe

3. What did Mrs Wonder get trapped in?

a) Tree sap

b) A cage

c) Ice

4. What did Flame accidentally set on fire?

a) A stuffed toy

b) A poster

c) A chair

5. What was Mrs Wonder's superpower?

a) Making fire

b) Making water

c) Stopping time

Turn over for answers

Book Bands for Guided Reading

The Institute of Education book banding system is a scale of colours that reflects the various levels of reading difficulty. The bands are assigned by taking into account the content, the language style, the layout and phonics. Word, phrase and sentence level work is also taken into consideration.

Maverick Early Readers are a bright, attractive range of books covering the pink to white bands. All of these books have been book banded for guided reading to the industry standard and edited by a leading educational consultant.

To view the whole Maverick Readers scheme, visit our website at www.maverickearlyreaders.com

Or scan the QR code above to view our scheme instantly!

Quiz Answers: 1c, 2a, 3c, 4c, 5c